Mr. Charles Dickens'

A Christmas Carol:

A Ghost Story of Christmas

Adapted for Readers' Theater

By Mr. Lance Davis

As Performed by Parson's Nose Theater

ABOUT THE PLAY

I held off doing "A Christmas Carol" at Parson's Nose for a number of years because there were so many good productions already being done, and I wasn't sure what Parson's Nose could offer that was unique. Then in 2008 the economy, and arts funding in particular, took a dive, and PNT had to reinvent its way of fulfilling its mission.

While I was a theater student at Notre Dame our wonderful Professor Fred Syburg introduced us to a fascinating form called Readers' Theater. It had originated in the 1930s in various forms, and been revived after World War II due to its emphasis on simplicity – actors reading wonderful works in front of an audience – no long rehearsals, no sets, no costumes, just "essential" theater – actor, text, audience and imagination.

PNT had something new to deliver to the local theater scene. We booked an intimate space – Jameson Brown Coffee in Pasadena - set up folding chairs, outlined a stage at one end of the room, and began a tradition.

The key attraction, as I said, is simplicity. It's a lot like radio. A friend called it "theater unplugged". The actors sit along the back of the stage, coming forward to play as needed. They hold their scripts, but are familiar enough with their lines to lift heads and make contact with their partners and the audience. The actors sing the carols and create the sound effects. A "thundersheet" can be bought at Home Depot for $10. We add another PNT touch in that our adaptation emphasizes our two narrators who drive the action of the play, emphasizing Dickens' delicious descriptions – the bits often overlooked when we were in school and had to have a hundred pages read by Monday, but are now able to savor, such as onions on grocer shelves winking at girls who pass by.

I hope you have fun. It's become a welcomed chance for our company and our audience to get together every year. It's always a mixed bag as to who's available, so there are inevitably fun assignments – women play men and vice versa (Mrs. Fezziwig), young play old and old play young. However it falls it brings us, by evening's end, into the spirit of Christmas. And we've brought our second-greatest English writer's work into the spotlight to boot.

I'd like to thank all those who make Parson's Nose so vibrant. Our professional company, our board, our volunteers, our donors – especially Terry Perl, Eileen Davis and Mario and Therese Molina – you, our audience without whom "live" theater would not be "live". And most especially my wife Mary Chalon and our daughter Jemma Davis. Merry Christmas. - LD

<u>The Company</u>

Actor 1 - Marley, Old Joe, Customer 1, Gentleman 2
Actor 2 - Bob Cratchit
Actor 3 - Narrator 2, Servant
Actor 4 - Fred
Actor 5 - Belle, Martha Cratchit, Turkey Boy
Actor 6 - Spirit 1, Merchant 2, Charwoman
Actor 7 - Narrator 1
Actor 8 - All Scrooges
Actor 9 - Girl Caroling. Fan, Mrs. Fred, Caroline, Laundress, Tiny Tim
Actor 10 - Spirit 2, Undertaker (just cackling), Gentleman 1
Actor 11 - Mrs. Cratchit
Actor 12 - Goodman 1, Fezziwig, Belle's Husband, Sailor 1, Merchant 1
Actor 13 - Goodman 2, Mrs. Fezziwig, Customer 2, Peter Cratchit, Sailor 2, Man
Stage Manager - Sound, Lights

Note: Please pay everyone something. It's Christmas.

PRESHOW: Cast sings: "Christmas is coming/The goose is getting fat/Please put a penny...etc."

ACT I

CAROL: IN THE BLEAK MIDWINTER

NARRATOR
Stave 1. Marley was dead, to begin with. There is no doubt whatever about that. The register of his burial was signed by the Clergyman, the Clerk, the Undertaker and the Chief Mourner. Scrooge signed it. You will therefore permit me to repeat, emphatically, that Marley was as dead as a door-nail.

SOUND: HAMMER ON PIPE

This must be distinctly understood or nothing wonderful can come of the story. If we were not perfectly convinced that Hamlet's Father died before the play began, there would be nothing remarkable in his taking a stroll at night to astonish his son's weak mind. Scrooge never painted out Marley's name above the warehouse door. The firm was known as "Scrooge and Marley". Sometimes people new to the business called Scrooge "Scrooge", and sometimes "Marley", but he answered to both names. It was all the same to him.

SCROOGE ENTERS SLOWLY

Oh! But he was a tight-fisted hand, Scrooge. A squeezing, wrenching, grasping, scraping, clutching, covetous old sinner. Hard and sharp as flint, and solitary as an oyster. The cold within him froze his old features, nipped his pointed nose, shriveled his cheek, stiffened his gait; made his eyes red, his thin lips blue; and spoke out shrewdly in his grating voice. Nobody ever stopped him in the street to say...

GOODMAN 1
My dear Scrooge, how are you? When will you come to see me?

NARRATOR 1
No beggars implored him to bestow a trifle. No children asked him what it was o'clock. Even the blind men's dogs appeared to know him, and when they saw him coming on, would tug their owners into doorways. But what did Scrooge care? It was the very thing he liked.

NARRATOR 2
Once upon a time -- of all the good days in the year, on Christmas Eve -- old Scrooge sat busy in his counting-house. It was cold, bleak, biting weather. The door of Scrooge's counting-house was open, that he might keep his eye upon his clerk, who, in a dismal little cell beyond, was copying letters. Scrooge had a very small fire, but the clerk's fire was so very much smaller that it looked like one coal. He couldn't replenish it, for Scrooge kept the coal-box in his own room; and so surely as the clerk came in with the shovel, the master predicted that it would be necessary for them to part. Wherefore the clerk put on his white comforter and tried to warm himself at the candle, in which effort, not being a man of a strong imagination, he failed.

SOUND: Dingaling. (Rather tinnish if possible)

FRED
A merry Christmas, Uncle! God save you!

NARRATOR 2
It was the voice of Scrooge's nephew.

SCROOGE
(dismissive) Bah. Humbug.

FRED
Christmas a humbug, Uncle? You don't mean that, I am sure.

SCROOGE
I do. Merry Christmas? What right have you to be merry? What
reason have you to be merry? You're poor enough.

FRED
Come, what right have you to be dismal? You're rich enough.

SCROOGE
Humbug!

FRED
Oh, don't be cross, Uncle.

SCROOGE
What else can I be when I live in such a world of fools as this? Out
upon merry Christmas. What's Christmas to you but a time for
paying bills without money; a time for finding yourself a year older,
but not an hour richer. If I could work my will, every idiot who goes
about with "Merry Christmas' on his lips, should be boiled in his
own pudding, and buried with a stake of holly through his heart.

FRED
Uncle!

SCROOGE
Nephew! Keep Christmas in your own way, and let me keep it in mine.

FRED
But you don't keep it.

SCROOGE
Let me leave it alone, then1 Much good may it do you! Much good it has ever done you!

CAROL: IT CAME UPON A MIDNIGHT CLEAR

FRED
There are many things, Uncle, from which I might have derived good, by which I have not profited, I dare say Christmas among the rest. But I have always thought of Christmas as the only time in the long calendar of the year when men and women seem, by one consent, to open their shut-up hearts freely, and to think of people below them as if they really were fellow-passengers to the grave, and not a race of creatures bound on other journeys. And therefore, uncle, though it has never put a scrap of gold in my pocket, I believe it has done me good, and will do me good; and I say, God bless it.

CAROL OUT

CRATCHIT hesitantly applauds, stops.

SCROOGE
Let me hear another sound from you, sir, and you'll keep your Christmas by losing your situation! (to Fred) You're quite a powerful speaker, sir. I wonder you don't go into Parliament.

FRED
Oh don't be angry, Uncle. Come, dine with us tomorrow.

SCROOGE
I will. I will. I will see you in hell first.

FRED
But why, Uncle? Why?

SCROOGE
Why did you get married?

FRED
Because I fell in love.

SCROOGE
You "fell in love." Good afternoon.

FRED
Nay, Uncle, you never came to see me before that happened. Why give it as a reason for not coming now? I want nothing from you; I ask nothing of you; why cannot we be friends?

SCROOGE
Good afternoon.

FRED
I am sorry, with all my heart, to find you so resolute. But I'll keep my Christmas humor to the last. And so, a Merry Christmas, Uncle! Good afternoon!

SCROOGE
Bah!

FRED
And a Happy New Year!

CRATCHIT
...good afternoon...

SCROOGE
Bah!

SOUND: Dingaling

There's another fellow, my clerk, with but fifteen shillings a week, a wife and family, talking about a merry Christmas! I'll retire to Bedlam!

NARRATOR 2
The clerk, in letting Scrooge's nephew out, let two people in.

GOODMAN 1
(jolly) "Scrooge and Marley's", I believe? Have I the pleasure of addressing Mr. Scrooge or Mr. Marley?

SCROOGE
Mr. Marley has been dead these seven years, sirs. He died seven years ago, this very night.

GOODMAN 2
Well, we have no doubt his liberality is well represented by his surviving partner?

AWKWARD SILENCE

GOODMAN 1
At this festive season of the year, Mr. Scrooge, it is more than usually desirable that we should make some slight provision for the Poor and Destitute, who suffer greatly at the present time. Many thousands are in want of common necessaries; hundreds of thousands are in want of common comforts.

SCROOGE
Are there no prisons?

GOODMAN 1
...er...plenty of prisons...

SCROOGE
And the union workhouses. They are still in operation?

GOODMAN 2
They are. I wish I could say they were not.

SCROOGE
The Poor Law is in full vigor, then?

GOODMAN 1
It is very busy, sir.

SCROOGE
Oh. I was afraid from what you said at first that something had occurred to stop them in their useful course. I'm very glad to hear it.

GOODMAN 2
Sir, a few of us are endeavoring to raise a fund to buy the poor some meat and drink and means of warmth. We choose this time because it is a time, of all others, when Want is keenly felt, and Abundance rejoices. Now, what shall we put you down for?

SCROOGE
Nothing.

GOODMAN 2
Of course. You wish to be anonymous?

SCROOGE
I wish to be left alone! Since you ask me what I wish, gentlemen, that is my answer. I do not "make merry" myself at Christmas, and I cannot afford to make idle people merry. I help to support the establishments I have mentioned - they cost enough - and those who are badly off must go there.

GOODMAN 1
Many can't go there, sir; and many would rather die.

SCROOGE
If they would rather die, they had better do it. And decrease the surplus population. It is not my business, sirs. It is enough for a man to

understand his own business and not to interfere with other people's. Mine occupies me constantly. Good afternoon.

NARRATOR 1
Seeing it would be useless to pursue their point, the gentlemen withdrew.

SOUND: DOORBELL
Scrooge resumed his labors with an improved opinion of himself, and in a more facetious temper than was usual with him.

SOUND: Distant CHURCH BELL

Meanwhile the fog and darkness thickened. The cold became intense. Piercing, searching, biting cold.

GIRL (NERVOUS)
"God rest ye, merry gentlemen, let nothing you dismay...'

SCROOGE
Humbug!

SILENCE.

NARRATOR 1
At length, the hour of shutting up the counting-house arrived. With an ill-will Scrooge dismounted from his stool, and tacitly admitted the fact to the expectant clerk, who instantly snuffed his candle out, and put on his hat.

SCROOGE
You'll want all day tomorrow, I suppose?

BOB CRATCHIT
If quite convenient, sir.

SCROOGE
It is not convenient, and it's not fair. If I was to keep half-a-crown for it, you'd think yourself ill-used, I'll be bound. And yet you don't think me ill-used, when I pay a day's wages for no work.

BOB CRATCHIT
But, sir, it's only once a year.

SCROOGE
A poor excuse for picking a man's pocket every twenty-fifth of
December. Be here all the earlier next morning.

BOB CRATCHIT
Yes, sir. Thank you, sir.

NARRATOR 1
The office was closed in a twinkling.

SOUND: Dingalink

And the clerk, with the long ends of his white comforter dangling
below his waist, went down a slide on Corn Hill at the end of a lane
of boys twenty times, in honor of it's being Christmas Eve…

SOUND: WHOOPS AND CALLS

…and then ran home to Camden Town as hard as he could pelt, to
play at Blind Man's Buff.

CAROL: MARY WALKED THROUGH A WOOD OF THORN

NARRATOR 2
Scrooge took his dinner and went home to bed.

SOUND: CHURCH BELLS DARK

He lived in chambers which had once belonged to his deceased
partner. A gloomy suite of rooms in a lowering pile of a building, up
a yard where it had so little business to be that one could scarcely
help fancying it must have run there when it was a young house,
playing at hide-and-seek with other houses, and forgotten its way out
again. Nobody lived in it but Scrooge.

NARRATOR 1
Now it is a fact that there was nothing at all particular about the knocker on the door, except it was very large. It is also a fact that Scrooge had seen it, night and morning.

NARRATOR 2
Also that Scrooge had as little of what is called "fancy" about him as any man in the city of London.

NARRATOR 1
Let it also be borne in mind that Scrooge had not bestowed one thought on Marley since his last mention of his dead partner that afternoon.

NARRATOR 2
And then let any man explain to me, if he can, how it happened that Scrooge, having his key in the lock of the door, saw in the knocker - not a knocker - but Marley's face!

SOUND: THUNDER SPRING

NARRATOR 1
Marley's face. It had a dismal light about it, like a bad lobster in a dark cellar. But as Scrooge looked fixedly at this phenomenon...it was a knocker again.

SOUND: THUNDER SPRING OUT

SCROOGE
Bah.

NARRATOR 2
He fastened the door, walked across the hall and up the stairs. Darkness is cheap and Scrooge liked it. But before he shut his door, he walked through his rooms. Nobody under the table, nobody under the sofa, nobody under the bed. Quite satisfied, he closed his door and locked himself in, put on his dressing-gown, slippers and nightcap, and sat down before the fire.

CAROL: MARY WALKED (REPRISE)

NARRATOR 2
The fireplace was an old one, built by some Dutch merchant, and paved all round with quaint Dutch tiles, designed to illustrate the Scriptures. There were Cains and Abels, Pharaoh's daughters, Queens of Sheba, Apostles putting off to sea in butter-boats.

SCROOGE
Humbug.

CAROL OUT

NARRATOR 2
His glance happened to rest upon a bell that hung in the room. And as he looked, this bell began to swing!

SOUND: SINGLE BELL
Soon it rang out loudly...and so did every bell in the house.

SOUND: SCARY BELLS
The bells ceased as they had begun.

SOUND: OUT!

BEAT.

SOUND: CHAINS

NARRATOR 1
They were succeeded by a clanking noise, deep down below; as if some person were dragging a heavy chain.

SOUND: CHAINS

SOUND: SOFT BASS DRUM - HEART BEAT
The cellar-door flew open..

SOUND: CELLAR DOOR CREAK
..and then he heard the noise much louder; then coming up the stairs; then coming straight towards his door.

SCROOGE
Bah. I don't believe it.

NARRATOR 2
His color changed though, when without a pause it came through the heavy door and passed into the room before his eyes.

SOUND: BASS DRUM. BOOM!

NARRATOR 1
Marley's ghost! The same face: the very same. Marley in his pigtail, waistcoat, tights and boots. The chain he drew was wound about him like a tail made of cash-boxes, keys, padlocks, and heavy purses. His body was transparent, so that Scrooge could see the two buttons on his coat behind. Scrooge had often heard it said that Marley had no bowels but he had never believed it until now.

SCROOGE
How now! What do you want with me?

MARLEY'S GHOST
…Much.

NARRATOR 1
Marley's voice, no doubt about it.

SCROOGE
Who are you?

MARLEY'S GHOST
Ask me who I was.

SCROOGE
Who were you then? You are particular, for a shade...

MARLEY'S GHOST
In life I was your partner, Jacob Marley. (BEAT) You don't believe in me.

SCROOGE
I don't.

MARLEY'S GHOST
Why do you doubt your senses?

SCROOGE
Because a little thing can affect them. You may be an undigested bit
of beef, a blot of mustard, a fragment of underdone potato. There's
more of gravy than of the grave about you, whatever you are...

MARLEY LETS OUT A CRY

SOUND: CHAINS -

NARRATOR 1
At this the spirit shook its chain with such a dismal and appalling
noise, that Scrooge held on tight to his chair to save himself from
falling in a swoon.

NARRATOR 2
But how much greater was his horror when the phantom, taking off
the bandage round its head, its lower jaw dropped down upon its
breast.

SOUND: "PLOP"

MARLEY'S GHOST
Man of the worldly mind! Do you believe in me or not?

SCROOGE
I do. I must. But why do spirits walk the earth, and why do they
come to me?

MARLEY'S GHOST
It is required of every man that the spirit within him should walk abroad among his fellow men and travel far and wide. And if that spirit goes not forth in life, it is condemned to do so after death. It is doomed to wander through the world - oh woe is me! - and witness what it cannot share but might have shared on earth, and turned to happiness.

SCROOGE
You - You are fettered, Jacob. Tell me why.

MARLEY'S GHOST
I wear the chain I forged in life. I made it link by link and yard by yard. I girded it on of my own free will. Is its pattern strange to you? Or would you know the weight and length of the strong coil you bear yourself? It was full as heavy and long seven Christmas Eves ago. And you have labored on it since. Oh, it is a ponderous chain.

SCROOGE
Oh, speak comfort to me, Jacob.

MARLEY'S GHOST
I have none to give. Nor can I tell you what I would. I cannot rest, I cannot linger anywhere. My spirit never walked beyond our counting-house. My spirit never roved beyond the narrow limits of our money-changing hole. And weary journeys lie before me.

SCROOGE
Seven years dead. And travelling all that time?

MARLEY'S GHOST
The whole time. No rest, no peace.

SCROOGE
You travel fast?

MARLEY'S GHOST
On the wings of the wind. Seven year! Captive, bound, and double-ironed!

SCROOGE
But you were a good man of business, Jacob...

MARLEY'S GHOST
Business? Mankind was my business! Charity, Mercy and
Benevolence were all my business. At this time of the year I suffer
most. Hear me! My time is nearly gone.
How it is that I appear before you I may not tell. I have sat invisible
beside you many and many a day...

NARRATOR 1
It was not an agreeable idea.

MARLEY'S GHOST
I am here tonight to warn you that you have yet a chance and hope
of escaping my fate. A chance and hope of my procuring.

SCROOGE
You were always a good friend, Jacob.

MARLEY'S GHOST
You will be haunted by Three Spirits.

SCROOGE
Is – is that the hope you mentioned, Jacob? I think I'd rather not.

MARLEY'S GHOST
Without their visits you cannot hope to shun the path I now tread.
Expect the First tomorrow, when the bell tolls One. Expect the
Second the next night at the same hour...

SCROOGE
Couldn't I take 'em all at once, and have it over?

MARLEY'S GHOST
The Third upon the next night at the last stroke of Twelve. Look to
see me no more. And look that, for your own sake, you remember
what has passed between us.

NARRATOR 1
When it had said these words, the specter took its kerchief from the table and bound it round its head, as before.

SOUND: "SHWUP!"

NARRATOR 2
The apparition walked backward from him; and at every step it took the window behind raised itself a little , till it was wide open.

SOUND: DISTANT WAILS

Scrooge became sensible of confused noises in the air; incoherent SOUNDs of lamentation and regret; wailings inexpressibly sorrowful. The Specter joined in the mournful dirge and floated out upon the bleak, dark night. Scrooge followed to the window.

SOUND: LOUDER

NARRATOR 1
The air was filled with phantoms, ghosts of "Departed Usurers", wandering hither and thither and moaning as they went. Every one wore chains. Some few were linked together. None were free. Many had been known to Scrooge. He had been quite familiar with one old ghost in a white waistcoat, with a monstrous iron Safe attached to its ankle, who cried piteously at being unable to assist a Wretched Woman with an Infant. The misery with them all was that they sought to interfere for Good in human matters, but had Lost the power forever.

NARRATOR 2
Whether these creatures faded into mist or mist enshrouded them, he could not tell. But they and their spirit voices faded together.

SOUND OUT.

NARRATOR 1
Scrooge closed the window. And being - from the emotion he had undergone, or his glimpse of the Invisible World - much in need of repose, went straight to bed without undressing, and fell asleep upon the instant!

NARRATOR 2
Stave Two.

SOUND: LAST OF TWELVE CHIMES

SCROOGE
Twelve o'clock? Impossible. Jacob Marley? Was it a dream? A "visitation" when the bell tolls One.

SOUND: DEEP GONG.

SPIRIT ONE appears

NARRATOR 2
It was a strange figure. Like a child, yet not so like a child as like an old man. It wore a tunic of purest white.

SCROOGE
Are you the Spirit whose coming was foretold to me?

SPIRIT ONE
I am. I am the Ghost of Christmas Past.

SCROOGE
What business brings you here?

SPIRIT ONE
Your welfare.

SCROOGE
Much obliged. Perhaps an unbroken rest might have served me better?

SPIRIT ONE
Your Reclamation, then. Rise, and walk with me.

NARRATOR 1
The spirit moved to the window.

SCROOGE
But the weather, the hour; I might fall.

SOUND: WIND

SPIRIT ONE
Bear but a touch of my hand and you shall be upheld in more than this.

(They almost touch hands)

CAROL: WHILE SHEPHERDS WATCHED THEIR FLOCKS

NARRATOR 1
As the words were spoken, they passed through the wall, and stood upon an open country road, with fields on either hand. It was a clear, cold, winter day, with snow upon the ground.

SCROOGE
Where are you leading me?

NARRATOR 1
He was conscious of a thousand odors floating in the air, each one connected with a thousand thoughts, and hopes long, long, forgotten.

SCROOGE
Good Heavens! (joyous) I was a boy here!

SPIRIT ONE
You remember the way?

SCROOGE
Remember? I could walk it blindfold.

SPIRIT ONE
Strange, to have forgotten it for so many years.

NARRATOR 1
They walked along the road, Scrooge recognizing every gate and post and tree, until a little market-town appeared in the distance, with its bridge, its church, and winding river. Some shaggy ponies now were seen trotting towards them with boys upon their backs, who called to other boys in country gigs driven by farmers. All were in great spirits and shouted to each other until the broad fields were so full of merry music that the crisp air laughed to hear it.

CAST
Merry Christmas! Merry Christmas

SCROOGE WAVES BUT NO RESPONSE

SPIRIT ONE
These are but Shadows of Things that have Been; they have no consciousness of us. The school is not quite deserted. A solitary child, neglected by his friends, is left there still.

SCROOGE
I know.

NARRATOR 2
They left the high-road and soon approached a mansion of dull, red brick. A large house of broken fortunes. Offices little used, windows broken. They entered the dreary hall to a door at the back. It opened before them and disclosed a long, bare, melancholy room, made barer still by lines of plain desks. At one of these, a lonely boy was reading near a feeble fire. And Scrooge sat down and wept. Suddenly a man, in foreign garments, wonderfully real, stood outside the window, with an axe in his belt, and leading an ass laden with wood.

SOUND: ARABIAN MUSIC

SCROOGE
Why, it's Ali Baba! Dear old Ali Baba! Yes, one Christmas time, when yonder child was left here all alone, he did come just like that. Poor boy! And Valentine, and his wild brother, Orson. And the Sultan's Groom turned upside down by the Genii. There he is! Serve him right! What business had he to be married to the Princess? Poor Robin Crusoe. Where have you been, Robin Crusoe? There goes Friday, running for his life! Halloa! Oh!

SOUND FADES OUT
I wish...

SPIRIT ONE
What?

SCROOGE
Nothing. There was a girl, singing at my door last night.

SPIRIT ONE
Let us see another Christmas.

NARRATOR 2
Scrooge's former self grew larger. The room became darker and more dirty. The panels shrunk, the windows cracked; fragments of plaster fell. There he was, alone again, while the other boys had gone home for the holidays. He was not reading now, but walking up and down. Scrooge glanced anxiously towards the door.

CAROL: LO, HOW A ROSE E'ER BLOOMING
It opened and a girl came darting in, and put her arms about his neck, and kissed him.

FAN
Dear, dear brother! I have come to bring you home, dear brother! To bring you home!

SCROOGE
Home? Home, little Fan?

FAN
Yes! Home, for good and all. Home, for ever and ever. Father is so much kinder than he used to be that home's like Heaven! He spoke so gently to me one night when I was going to bed that I was not afraid to ask him if you might come home. And he said yes, you should! And sent me in a coach to bring you. And you are never to come back here. But first we're to be together all the Christmas long, and have the merriest time in all the world!

SCROOGE
You are quite a woman, little Fan.

SHE FADES AWAY

SPIRIT ONE
A delicate creature. But she had a large heart.

SCROOGE
So she had. I will not gainsay it, Spirit.

SPIRIT ONE
She died a woman, and had, as I think, children?

SCROOGE
One child. Fred.

NARRATOR 2
Although they had but at that moment left the school behind them they were now in the busy thoroughfares of a city.

SOUND: CARRIAGES, CITY

It was evening and the streets were lighted up. The Ghost stopped at a warehouse door.

SOUND OUT

SCROOGE
Was I - was I 'prenticed here?

NARRATOR 2
They went in. The sight of a gentleman in a Welsh wig, sitting behind a high desk.

SCROOGE
Why, it's old Fezziwig! Bless his heart! It's Fezziwig alive again!

FEZZIWIG
Yo ho, there! Ebenezer? Dick?

NARRATOR 1
Scrooge's former self, now grown a young man, came briskly in accompanied by his fellow-'prentice.

SCROOGE
Dick Wilkins, to be sure!

FEZZIWIG
No more work tonight, boys! Christmas Eve, Dick! Christmas, Ebenezer! Shutters up!

CAROL: DECK THE HALLS -

NARRATOR 2
They charged into the street with the shutters; had them up in their places; barred them and pinned them and came back panting like race-horses.

FEZZIWIG
Hilli-ho! Clear away, lads!

NARRATOR 2
There was nothing they wouldn't have cleared away. It was done in a minute. The floor was swept, the lamps trimmed, fuel heaped upon the fire, and the warehouse was as snug and warm and bright a ballroom as you would desire to see upon a winter's night.

MUSIC: FIDDLE

SOUNDS: AD LIBS ACCORDING TO DESCRIPTIONS

NARRATOR 1

In came a Fiddler and went up to the desk and made an orchestra of it and tuned like fifty stomach-aches. In came Mr. Fezziwig, one vast, substantial Smile. In came the three Miss Fezziwigs, beaming and lovable. In came the six young Followers, whose hearts they broke. In came all the Young Men and Women employed in the business. In came the Housemaid, with her cousin, the Baker. In came the Cook, with her brother's particular friend, the Milkman. In came "The Boy from over the Way'. In they all came; some shyly, some boldly, some gracefully, some awkwardly. Away they all went, twenty couple at once.

NARRATOR 2

There were Dances and there were Forfeits and more Dances, and there was Cake and there was Negus and there was Cold Roast, and there was Cold Boiled, and there were Mince-Pies and plenty of Beer. But the great effect of the evening came when the fiddler struck up "Sir Roger de Coverley."

MUSIC: CHANGE TO "SIR ROGER DE COVERLY"

Then Old Fezziwig stood out, to dance with Mrs. Fezziwig. As to her, she was worthy to be his partner in every sense of the term. And if that's not high praise, tell me higher and I shall use it. A positive Light appeared to issue from Fezziwig's calves. They shone in every part of the dance like moons. And when Old Fezziwig and Mrs. Fezziwig had gone all through the dance: Advance and Retire, Both Hands to Partner, Bow and Curtsey, Thread-the-Needle and Back Again; Fezziwig Cut-Cut so deftly that he appeared to wink with his legs.

NARRATOR 1

When the clock struck eleven this domestic ball broke up.

MUSIC: SOFTENS

Mr. and Mrs. Fezziwig took their stations, one on either side of the door and, shaking hands with every person individually as he or she went out,

SOUND: AD LIBS "THANK YOU, SIR. MERRY CHRISTMAS, MUM."

wished him or her a "Merry Christmas". And thus the Cheerful Voices died away.

MUSIC FADES. CAST FADES AWAY

SPIRIT ONE
A small matter. To make these silly folk so full of Gratitude.

SCROOGE
Small?

SPIRIT ONE
Is it not? He has spent but a few pounds of your mortal money. Is that so much that he deserves such praise?

SCROOGE
Bah! It isn't that, Spirit. Why, he has the power to render us happy or unhappy. His power lies in words and looks. The happiness he gives is quite as great as if it cost a fortune. Why --

SPIRIT ONE
What is the matter?

SCROOGE
Nothing. I should like to be able to say a word to my clerk just now, that's all.

SOUND: WIND - CAST

NARRATOR 1
Scrooge and the Ghost again stood in the open air.

SPIRIT ONE
My time grows short.

NARRATOR 1
Again Scrooge saw himself. He was older now, a man in the prime of life. His face had begun to wear the signs of Care and Avarice. There was an restless motion in the eye.

NARRATOR 2
He was not alone, but sat by the side of a fair young girl, in whose eyes there were tears.

BELLE
It matters little to you, very little. Another idol has displaced me. And if it can cheer and comfort you in time to come, as I would have tried to do, I have no cause to grieve.

YOUNG SCROOGE
What idol has displaced you?

BELLE
A golden one.

YOUNG SCROOGE
Belle! Such is the even-handed dealing of the world. There is nothing on which it is so hard as Poverty, yet there is nothing it condemns with such severity as the pursuit of Wealth.

BELLE
You fear the world too much, Ebenezer. I have seen your nobler aspirations fall off, one by one, until the master- passion, Gain, engrosses you.

YOUNG SCROOGE
And if I have grown, what then? I am not changed towards you. Am I?

BELLE
Our contract is an old one. It was made when we were both poor, and content to be so until we could improve our worldly fortune by our patient industry. You are changed. When it was made, you were another man.

YOUNG SCROOGE
Man? I was a boy.

BELLE
Your own feeling tells you that you were not what you now are. I am.
That which promised happiness when we were One in Heart, is fraught
with misery now that we are Two. How often and how keenly I have
thought of this I will not say. It is enough that I have thought of it...and
can release you.

YOUNG SCROOGE
Belle! Have I ever sought release?

BELLE
In words? No.

YOUNG SCROOGE
In what, then?

BELLE
In a changed nature, an altered spirit; in everything that made my love of
any worth or value in your sight. Tell me. If this had never been between
us, would you seek me out, a dowerless girl, and try to win me now?
(Beat) No.

YOUNG SCROOGE
You think not...

BELLE
Heaven knows I would gladly think otherwise if I could. I release you,
Ebenezar, with a full heart. For the love of him you once were. You may -
- the memory of what is past half makes me hope you will have pain in
this. A very brief time. And then you will dismiss the recollection of it
gladly, as an Unprofitable Dream from which it happened well that you
awoke. May you be happy in the life you have Chosen.

BELLE FADES.

SCROOGE
Spirit! Show me no more!

SPIRIT ONE
One Shadow more.

SOUND: WIND

NARRATOR 2
They were in another place. A room, not large or handsome, but full of Comfort. Near the winter fire sat a beautiful young girl, so like that last that Scrooge believed it was the same, until he saw *her*, now a comely matron, sitting opposite...her daughter. The noise in the room was perfectly tumultuous

SOUND: CHILDREN ANTICIPATING FATHER

for there were more children there than Scrooge could count, and they were not forty children conducting themselves like one, but every child was conducting itself like forty. (KNOCK) A knocking at the door was heard - The Father, who came home laden with Christmas toys and presents. Then the shouting and the struggling and the onslaught that was made! To dive into his pockets, despoil him of brown-paper parcels, hug him round his neck and kick his legs in irrepressible affection.

SOUND "Father! Father!" FADES

Scrooge looked on more attentively than ever when the Master of the house, his daughter leaning fondly on him, sat with her and her mother at his own fireside. And when Scrooge thought that such another Creature, quite as graceful and as full of promise, might have called *him* "Father', and been a springtime in the haggard winter of his life, his sight grew very dim indeed.

BELLE'S HUSBAND (SMILING)
Belle, I saw an old friend of yours this afternoon.

BELLE
Who was it?

BELLE'S HUSBAND
Guess!

BELLE
How can I? Tut, don't I know. (warmly) Mr. Scrooge?

BELLE'S HUSBAND
Mr. Scrooge it was. I passed his office window, and there he sat. Quite alone in the world, I do believe.

SCROOGE
Spirit, remove me from this place.

SPIRIT ONE
These were Shadows of things that have been. That they are what they are, do not blame me.

SCROOGE
Haunt me no longer!

NARRATOR 2
Scrooge observed that the Spirit's light was burning high and bright, and dimly connecting that with its influence over him, he seized the extinguisher-cap and by a sudden action pressed it down upon its head. But though Scrooge pressed it down with all his force he could not hide the light which streamed from under it in an unbroken flood upon the ground. He was conscious of being exhausted, in his own bedroom. He had barely time to reel to bed before he sank into a heavy sleep.

NARRATOR 1
Stave 3.

SOUND: CLOCK CHIME

SOUND: GONG

SCROOGE WAKES. LOOKS ABOUT.

NARRATOR 2
Now Scrooge was ready for a broad field of strange Appearances. Nothing between a baby and a rhinoceros would have astonished him. But, being prepared for almost Anything, he was not by any means prepared for Nothing. And, consequently, when the clock struck One and no Shape appeared but only a ghostly Light, he was taken with a violent fit of Trembling.

SCROOGE
Strange. Where is it coming from?

NARRATOR 2
He began to think that the source and secret of the light might be in the adjoining room, from whence it seemed to shine. He got up softly and shuffled in his slippers to the door.

SPIRIT TWO (BOOMING)
Enter, Scrooge!

CAROL: WE THREE KINGS!

NARRATOR 1
It was his own room, there was no doubt about that. But it had undergone a surprising transformation. The walls and ceiling were so hung with living green that it looked a perfect Grove, from every part of which bright gleaming Berries glistened. Crisp leaves of holly, mistletoe, and ivy reflected back the light as if so many little Mirrors had been scattered there, and a mighty blaze went roaring up the chimney.

NARRATOR 2
Heaped on the floor, to form a kind of Throne, were turkeys, geese, game, poultry, great joints of meat, sucking-pigs...

NARRATOR 1
Wreaths of sausages!

NARRATOR 2
Mince-Pies!

NARRATOR 1
Plum-Puddings!

NARRATOR 2
Barrels of Oysters!

NARRATOR 1
Red-hot Chestnuts!

NARRATOR 2
Cherry-cheeked Apples!

NARRATOR 1
Juicy Oranges!

NARRATOR 2
Luscious Pears!

NARRATOR 1
Immense Twelfth-Cakes!

BOTH
And seething Bowls of Punch that made the chamber dim with their Steam!

SOUND: HSSSSSS!

NARRATOR 2
In easy state upon this couch, there sat a jolly Giant, glorious to see, who bore a glowing torch, in shape not unlike Plenty's Horn, and held it up, high up, to shed its light on Scrooge.

SPIRIT TWO (BEAMING)

Come in, man! And know me better! I am the Ghost of Christmas Present!

NARRATOR 2
It was clothed in one simple green robe, bordered with white fur. Its feet were bare and on its head it wore no other covering than a holly wreath set with shining icicles.

SPIRIT TWO
You have never seen the like of me before?

SCROOGE
Never.

SPIRIT TWO
Never walked with the younger members of my family?

SCROOGE
I don't think I have. Have you had many brothers, Spirit?

SPIRIT TWO
More than eighteen hundred!

SCROOGE
A tremendous family. Spirit, conduct me where you will. I went forth last night and learnt a lesson. If you have aught to teach me, let me profit by it.

SPIRIT TWO
Touch my robe!

NARRATOR 1
Scrooge did as he was told, and held it fast, and they stood in the city streets on Christmas morning.

SOUND: CARRIAGES

SOUND: LAUGHTER, ADLIBS

The sky was gloomy, and yet was there an air of cheerfulness abroad...

SOUND: CHATTER, SHOVELING

...for the people shoveling away on the housetops were jovial and full of glee, calling out to one another, and now and then exchanging a facetious snowball -- laughing heartily if it went right, and not less heartily if it went wrong. The Poulterers shops were still open and the Fruiterers were radiant in their glory. There were great, round, pot-bellied baskets of Chestnuts, shaped like the waistcoats of jolly old gentlemen, lolling at the doors and tumbling out into the street.

NARRATOR 2
There were ruddy, brown-faced Onions, winking from their shelves in wanton slyness at the Girls as they went by and glanced demurely at the hung-up Mistletoe.

NARRATOR 1
There were pears and apples clustered high in blooming Pyramids.

NARRATOR 2
There were bunches of Grapes.

NARRATOR 1
There were piles of fFlberts.

NARRATOR 2
There were Norfolk Biffins, squab and swarthy, setting off the yellow of the oranges and lemons, and urgently entreating to be carried home in paper bags.

NARRATOR 1
And the Grocers! Oh the Grocers! It was not alone that the scales descending on the counter made a merry sound...

NARRATOR 2
Or that the twine and roller parted company so briskly...

NARRATOR 1
Or that the blended scents of tea and coffee were so grateful to the nose...

NARRATOR 2
Or that the raisins were so plentiful...

NARRATOR 1
The almonds so extremely white...

NARRATOR 2
The sticks of cinnamon so long and straight...

NARRATOR 1
The candied fruits so caked and spotted with molten Sugar!

CAST
Mmmmmm!

NARRATOR 2
And the Customers, all so eager they tumbled up against each other at the door, crashing their wicker baskets wildly, and left their purchases upon the counter and came running back to fetch them, and committed hundreds of the like mistakes, in the best humour possible.

SOUND: CHURCH BELLS WARM

NARRATOR 2
And soon the steeples called good people all to church and chapel, and away they came, flocking through the streets in their best clothes and their gayest faces. And at the same time there emerged from scores of bye-streets innumerable people carrying their dinners to the bakers shops. These poor revelers appeared to interest the Spirit very much, for he stood with Scrooge in a baker's doorway, and taking off the covers as their bearers passed, sprinkled incense on their dinners from his torch.

SOUND: SLEIGH BELLS

It was a very uncommon kind of torch, for once or twice when there were angry words between some dinner-carriers who had jostled each other...

CUSTOMER 1
(gruffly) What! I beg your pardon!

CUSTOMER 2
(gruffly) I beg your pardon! You, sir...

NARRATOR 2
...he shed a few drops on them...

SOUND: SLEIGH BELLS

NARRATOR 2
...and their good humor was restored.

CUSTOMER 1
(beaming) After you, my good man!

CUSTOMER 2
(beaming) No, no, no, Sir, after you!

NARRATOR 2
For they said it was a shame to quarrel upon Christmas Day. And so it was. God love it, so it was.

SCROOGE
Spirit, is there a peculiar flavor in what you sprinkle from your torch?

SPIRIT TWO
There is. My own.

SCROOGE
Would it apply to any kind of dinner on this day?

SPIRIT TWO
To any Kindly given. To a Poor one most.

SCROOGE
Why to a poor one most?

SPIRIT TWO
Because it Needs it most.

CAROL: WHAT CHILD IS THIS

NARRATOR 1
They went on, invisible, into the Suburbs of the town, to Scrooge's
clerk's. And on the threshold of the door the Spirit smiled and
stopped, to bless Bob Cratchit's dwelling. Bob had but fifteen Bob
a-week himself. He pocketed on Saturdays but fifteen copies of his
Christian name. And yet the Ghost of Christmas Present blessed his
four-roomed house.

NARRATOR 2
Then up rose Mrs. Cratchit, dressed out but poorly in a twice-turned
Gown, but brave in Ribbons which are cheap, and make a goodly
show for sixpence. And she laid the cloth, assisted by Belinda
Cratchit, second of her daughters, also brave in Ribbons, while
Master Peter Cratchit plunged a fork into the saucepan of Potatoes.
And now two smaller Cratchits, boy and girl, came tearing in,
screaming that outside the Baker's they had smelt the Goose, and
known it for their own!

MRS. CRATCHIT
Whatever 'as got yor precious father then? An' yor brother, Tiny
Tim? And Martha warn't as late last Christmas Day by 'alf-an-'our!

MARTHA CRATCHIT
'ere's Martha, muvver!

MRS. CRATCHIT
Why, bless yor 'eart, my dear, 'ow late you are!

MARTHA CRATCHIT
We'd a deal of work t' finish up last night, and 'ad to clear away 'is
mornin'.

MRS. CRATCHIT
Well never mind so long as you're come. Sit down 'fore the fire, m' dear, and 'ave a warm.

PETER CRATCHIT
No, no! 'ere's father comin'! Hide, Martha, hide!

NARRATOR 1
So Martha hid herself, and in came Bob, the Father, with three feet of comforter hanging down before him, his threadbare clothes darned up and brushed, and Tiny Tim upon his shoulder. Tiny Tim bore a little crutch, and his limbs supported by an iron frame.

BOB CRATCHIT
Why, where's our Martha?

MRS. CRATCHIT
No' comin', Father.

BOB CRATCHIT
No' comin'? No' comin' on Christmas Day?

NARRATOR 2
Martha didn't like to see him disappointed, even if it were only in joke, so she came out from behind the closet door and ran into his arms, and young Peter bore Tiny Tim off into the wash-house that he might hear the Pudding singing in the Copper.

MRS. CRATCHIT
An' 'ow did Tim behive?

BOB CRATCHIT
As good as gold, and better. 'e gets thoughtful, sittin' by 'imself so much; and thinks the strangest things y' ever heard. 'e told me, comin' 'ome, that 'e hoped the people saw 'im in the church, because 'e was a cripple, an' it might be pleasant to them t' remember on Christmas Day who made lame beggars walk, an' blind men see.

NARRATOR 2
The young Cratchits went to the bakery to fetch the goose, and soon returned in high Procession. Such a bustle ensued that you might have thought a goose the rarest of all birds. Mrs. Cratchit made the gravy; Master Peter mashed the potatoes; Miss Belinda sweetened the apple-sauce; Martha dusted the plates. Bob took Tiny Tim beside him in a tiny corner of the table, and the two young Cratchits set chairs for everybody. At last the dishes were set, and grace was said.

CAST
Amen.

NARRATOR 1
It was succeeded by a breathless pause, as Mrs. Cratchit, after looking slowly all along the carving-knife, prepared to plunge it into the breast. And when she did...

CAST
Ooooooh!

BOB CRATCHIT
There never was such a goose! I don't believe there ever was such a goose!

NARRATOR 1
Its Tenderness and Flavor, Size and Cheapness, were the themes of universal admiration. Eked out by apple-sauce and mashed potatoes it was sufficient dinner for the whole family, and the Youngest Cratchits in particular were steeped in sage and onion.

NARRATOR 2
And now Mrs. Cratchit left the room alone, too nervous to bear witnesses, to take the pudding up and bring it in. Hallo! With a great deal of steam, like a speckled cannon-ball, blazing in ignited brandy, and with Christmas holly stuck into the top.

BOB CRATCHIT
A wonderful pudding, my dearest! Your greatest success since our marriage.

MRS. CRATCHIT
Coo!

NARRATOR 2
Nobody thought it was at all a Small pudding for a Large family. It would have been Heresy to do so.

NARRATOR 1
At last the dinner was done, the cloth cleared, apples and oranges put upon the table, and a shovel-full of Chestnuts on the fire. And all the family drew round the hearth.

BOB CRATCHIT
A Merry Christmas to us all, my dears. God bless us.

TINY TIM
God bless us, every One.

NARRATOR 2
Tim sat very close to his father's side upon his little stool, and Bob held his withered little hand in his.

SCROOGE
Spirit. Tell me...if Tiny Tim will live.

SPIRIT TWO
I see a Vacant Seat in the chimney-corner, and a Crutch without an owner. If these shadows remain unaltered, the child will die.

SCROOGE
No! Say he will be spared.

SPIRIT TWO
"If he be like to die, he had better do it, and decrease the surplus population."

BEAT.

BOB CRATCHIT (TOAST)
I give you Mr. Scrooge, the founder o' the feast.

MRS. CRATCHIT
Founder o' the feast indeed. I wish I 'ad him 'ere. I'd give 'im a piece of my mind to feast upon.

BOB CRATCHIT
My dear, the children. Christmas Day.

MRS. CRATCHIT
It must be Christmas Day on which one drinks the health of such an unfeeling man as Mr. Scrooge. You know 'e is, Robert. Christmas Day. I'll drink 'is health for your sake, not for 'is. A merry Christmas and a happy new year.

CAROL: COVENTRY CAROL

NARRATOR 2
They were not a handsome family. They were not well dressed. Their shoes were far from water-proof. Their clothes were scanty. But, they were happy. Grateful. Pleased with one another. And when they faded, Scrooge had his eye upon them, and especially on Tiny Tim, until the last.

NARRATOR 1
Intermission...

ACT II

CAROL: COVENTRY CAROL

NARRATOR 2
By this time it was getting dark, and snowing heavily. And as Scrooge and the Spirit went along the streets the brightness of the roaring Fires in Kitchens and Parlors was wonderful. Here, the flickering of the blaze showed preparations for a cozy Dinner.

NARRATOR 1
There, all the Children of the house were running out into the Snow to meet their married sisters, brothers, cousins, uncles, and aunts.

NARRATOR 2
Here, were Guests assembling.

NARRATOR 1
And there, a group of handsome Girls, all hooded and fur-booted, all chattering at once, tripped lightly off to some neighbor's house, where woe upon the Single Man who saw them enter - artful Witches, well they knew it - in a Glow!

SOUND: THUNDER SHEET

SOUND: WIND HOWLING

NARRATOR 2
And now, without a word of warning, they stood upon a Desert Moor, where masses of rude stone were cast about, as though it were the burial-place of giants.

SCROOGE
What place is this?

SPIRIT TWO
Where miners live, who labor in the bowels of the earth. They know me.

NARRATOR 2
A light shone from the window of a Hut. Passing through the wall of mud and stone..

SOUND: WIND OUT

...they found a cheerful company assembled round a glowing fire. An old man and woman, with their children and their children's children, and another generation beyond that, all decked out in their holiday attire. They were singing a Christmas song, and all joined in the chorus.

CAROL: O HOLY NIGHT

NARRATOR 1
The Spirit did not tarry here...

SOUND: SEA CRASHING

SOUND: THUNDER SPRING

SCROOGE
Whoooa! Not to sea, Spirit! Not to sea? A lighthouse?

SOUND: DRUM, WIND

OLD SAILOR I (SHOUTING)
Merry Christmas!

OLD SAILOR II
What's that?

OLD SAILOR I
I said "Merry Christmas'!

OLD SAILOR II
WHAT?

OLD SAILOR I
MERRY CHRISMAS!

OLD SAILOR II
OH! MERRY CHRISTMAS!

OLD SAILOR I
Good King Wenceslaus looked out...

OLD SAILOR II
On the feast of Stephen...

BOTH
When the snow lay 'round about/ Deep and crisp and even

SOUND: BASS DRUM

NARRATOR 2
Again the Ghost sped on, above the black and heaving, until far away from any shore they lighted on a ship. They stood beside the Helmsman at the wheel, the Look-out in the bow, the Officers who had the watch. Dark, ghostly figures in their several stations, but every man among them hummed a Christmas tune, or had a Christmas thought, or spoke to his Companion of some bygone Christmas Day, with Homeward Hopes belonging to it. And every man on board, waking or sleeping, good or bad, had a kinder word for another on that day than on any day in the year, and remembered those he cared for at a distance, and had known that They remembered Him.

SOUND: WAVES OUT

MUSIC: FIDDLE

SOUND: LAUGHTER

SOUND: FRED'S LAUGH OVER

NARRATOR 1
It was a great surprise to Scrooge to hear a hearty laugh. It was a much greater surprise for Scrooge to recognize it as his nephew's, and to find himself in a bright, dry, gleaming room. And if you should happen, by any unlikely chance, to know a man more blest in a Laugh than Scrooge's nephew, all I can say is, I should like to know him too.

FRED
It's true! He said Christmas was "a humbug", as I live! He believed it too!

MRS. FRED
Well more shame for him, Fred.

NARRATOR 2
Scrooge's niece. Bless those women. They never do anything by halves. They are always in earnest.

FRED
He is a comical old fellow, and not so pleasant as he might be. However, his offences carry their own punishment, and I'm sure I have nothing to say against him.

MRS. FRED
And I'm sure he's very rich. At least you always tell me so.

FRED
Yes, my dear, but his wealth is of no use to him. He don't do any good with it.

MRS. FRED
Well I have no patience with him.

FRED
Oh, I have. I'm sorry for him, and couldn't be angry with him if I tried. Who suffers by his ill whims? Himself, always. If he takes it into his head to dislike us, and won't come and dine with us, what's the consequence? True, he don't lose much of a dinner...

MRS. FRED
Indeed? I think he loses a very good dinner!

SOUND: LAUGHTER

FRED
And I'm very glad to hear it. And I mean to give him the same chance
every year whether he likes it or not. He may rail at Christmas till he dies,
but he can't help thinking better of it if he finds me going there, in good
temper, year after year, saying "Uncle Scrooge, how are you?" And if it
only puts him in the vein to leave his poor clerk fifty pounds that's
something.

MUSIC: "SIR ROGER DE COVERLY"

NARRATOR 1
After tea they had more Music and played "Forfeits", for it is good to be
children sometimes, and never better than at Christmas, when its mighty
Founder was a Child Himself. There was "Blind Man's Buff" and
Mistletoe. Scrooge begged like a boy to be allowed to stay until the guests
departed.

SCROOGE
One half hour, Spirit?

NARRATOR 1
It was a game called "Yes and No", where Scrooge's nephew had to think
of something, and the rest must find out what; he only answering "yes" or
"no". An animal? A live animal? A disagreeable animal? A savage animal?
An animal that growled and grunted? And lived in London? And walked
the streets? But was not a horse, or an ass, or a cow, or a bull, or a tiger, or
a dog, or a pig, or a cat, or a bear?

MRS. FRED
Fred! I know! It's your Uncle Scrooge!

SOUND: LAUGHTER

FRED
Well he has given us plenty of merriment this day, and it would be ungrateful not to drink his health. To my Uncle Scrooge.

CAST
Uncle Scrooge.

CAROL: COVENTRY CAROL
Lullay, Thou little tiny Child/ By, by, lully, lullay.
Lullay, Thou little tiny Child./ By, by, lully, lullay.
Then woe is me, poor Child, for Thee/And ever mourn and say;
For Thy parting, nor say nor sing / By, by, lully, lullay.

NARRATOR 2
The scene passed in the breath of the last word and they were again upon their travels. It was a long night, and strange, too, in that while Scrooge remained unaltered in his outward form, the Ghost grew older.

SCROOGE
Are spirits' lives so short?

SPIRIT TWO
My life is brief. It ends tonight.

SOUND: CHURCH BELLS - DARK

SCROOGE
Forgive me. I see something Strange protruding from your skirt. Is that a foot? Or... a claw?!

SPIRIT TWO
Look. Here.

NARRATOR 1
From the foldings of its robe, it brought two children. Wretched. Hideous.

SOUND: THUNDER SPRING

NARRATOR 2
A Boy and a Girl. Yellow, ragged, wolfish. Where Youth should have filled their features a stale and shrivelled Hand had pinched and twisted them. Where Angels might have sat, enthroned Devils lurked, and glared out, menacing.

SCROOGE
Are...they yours?

SPIRIT TWO
They are Mankind's. The boy is Ignorance. The girl is Want. Beware them both, but most beware the boy, for on his brow I see that written which is "Doom".

SCROOGE
Have they no refuge?

SPIRIT TWO
"Are there no prisons? Are there no workhouses?"

SOUND: CHURCH BELLS SOLEMN

NARRATOR 1
Stave 4. Scrooge lifted his eyes and beheld a solemn Phantom.

SOUND: BASS DRUM

It was shrouded in a deep black Garment, which concealed its head, its face, its form, and left nothing of it visible save one outstretched Hand.

SCROOGE
I am in the presence of the Ghost of Christmas Yet To Come? Oh Spirit, I fear you more than any spectre I have seen. But as I know your purpose is to do me good I am prepared to bear you company. Will you not speak to me? Lead on.

NARRATOR 2
The Phantom moved away.

SOUND: CARRIAGES

The city seemed to spring up about them. They were on the
Exchange, amongst the merchants.

MERCHANT 1
No, I don't know much about it. I only know he's dead.

MERCHANT 2
When did he die?

MERCHANT 1
Last night, I believe.

MERCHANT 2
I thought he'd never die. What was the matter with him?

MERCHANT 1
Lord knows.

MERCHANT 2
What has he done with his money?

MERCHANT 1
Hasn't left it to me; that's all I know. It'll be a cheap funeral, for
upon my life I don't know of anybody to go to it.

MERCHANT 2
I don't mind going, if a lunch is provided. But I must be fed.

NARRATOR 1
The Phantom glided on into a street. Its finger pointed to two
persons.

GENTLEMAN 1
How are you?

GENTLEMAN 2
How are you?

GENTLEMAN 1
Well Old Scratch got his own at last, hey?

GENTLEMAN 2
So I'm told. Cold, isn't it?

GENTLEMAN 1
Christmas. You're not a skater, I suppose?

GENTLEMAN 2
No. No.

GENTLEMAN 1
Good morning!

GENTLEMAN 2
Good morning!

NARRATOR 2
Scrooge was surprised that the Spirit should attach importance to conversations so trivial. They left and went into an obscure part of the town; the ways foul and narrow. Alleys and archways like so many cesspools.

NARRATOR 1
Far in this den there was a low-browed, Beetling shop, where old rags, bottles, bones, and greasy offal were bought. Upon the floor were piled heaps of rusty keys, nails, chains. Sitting in among the wares he dealt in was Old Joe.

ENTER CHARWOMAN AND LAUNDRESS.

ALL CACKLE.

CHARWOMAN
Let the Charwoman to be the first! Let the Laundress to be the
second! Look here, Old Joe, here's a chance!

OLD JOE
Y' couldn't have met in a better place. Come into the parlor. Ha ha!
We're all suitable to our calling. Come into the parlor.

NARRATOR 2
The woman who had spoken threw her bundle on the floor.

CHARWOMAN
What odds 'en, Mrs. Dilber? Ev'ry person 'as a right t' take care of
'emselves.

OLD JOE
'e always did!

LAUNDRESS
'at's true, indeed! No man more so!

CHARWOMAN
Who's the wiser, eh?

LAUNDRESS
None, indeed!

CHARWOMAN
Who's the worse for the loss of a few things? Not a dead man, eh?

LAUNDRESS
No, indeed. If he wanted to keep 'em after he was dead, the old
screw, why wasn't he natural in his lifetime? If 'e 'ad been, he'd have
'ad somebody t' look after him when he was struck, 'stead of gasping
out 'is last all alone.

CHARWOMAN
Truest word 'at ever was spoke. It's a judgment on him, it is.

LAUNDRESS
Open that bundle, Joe, and let me know the value of it. Speak out plain now.

NARRATOR 2
It was not extensive. A seal or two, a pencil-case, a pair of sleeve-buttons...

OLD JOE
...sheets, towels, two silver teaspoons, sugar tongs. Well 'ere you are, then. I always give too much to ladies. It's a weakness of mine. 'at's on your account.

CHARWOMAN
Now my bundle, Joe.

NARRATOR 1
Joe dragged out her large and heavy roll.

OLD JOE
What d'you call this then? 'is bed curtains? You don't mean to say you took 'em down, wif 'im still lyin' there?

CHARWOMAN
Yes I do. And why not?

OLD JOE
Ha ha! You were born to make your fortune, and you'll certainly do it.

CHARWOMAN
I shan't hold back my hand when I can get anythin' by reaching it out. Now don't drop that wax on his blankets...

OLD JOE
'is blankets?!

CHARWOMAN
Whose else? 'e isn't likely to take cold anymore, is 'e.

OLD JOE
I 'ope he didn't die of anyfing catching?

CHARWOMAN
Don't you be afraid of that. I ain't so fond of 'is company what I'd
loiter about 'im. And you may look through that shirt till your eyes
ache but you won't find a 'ole in it. They'd have wasted it, if it hadn't
been for me.

OLD JOE
What do you call wasting it?

CHARWOMAN
Putting it on him to be buried in! Somebody was fool enough to do
it! But I took it off 'im agin. Ahaha!

ALL CACKLE AND EXIT.

SCROOGE
I see, Spirit. The case of this unhappy man might be my own.
Merciful Heaven.

NARRATOR 1
The Phantom spread its dark robe before him like a wing, and
withdrawing it, revealed a Room.

CAROLINE PACING. MAN ENTERS.

CAROLINE
Is it good or bad?

MAN
Bad.

CAROLINE
We're ruined?

MAN
There's hope yet, Caroline.

CAROLINE
If he relents, nothing is past hope.

MAN
He's past relenting, my dear. He's dead.

CAROLINE
Thank God….Oh! Forgive me.

MAN
What the woman said was true. He was not only ill, but dying.

CAROLINE
To whom will our debt be transferred?

MAN
I don't know. But before that time we'll be ready with the money. And even were we not, it would be bad fortune indeed to find so merciless a creditor in his Successor. We may sleep tonight with light hearts, Caroline.

CAROLINE
Yes.

SCROOGE
Oh, Spirit, let me see some Tenderness connected with death!

NARRATOR 2
The Ghost conducted him through several streets. They entered Bob Cratchit's house, and found Peter reading to the Mother and Children seated round the fire.

PETER
"And he took a child, and set him in the midst of them."

SCROOGE
Where have I heard those words?

MRS. CRATCHIT
Oh this color hurts my eyes. And I wouldn't show weak eyes to your father when he comes home. It must be near his time now.

PETER
Past it, mother. I think he walks a little slower than he used, these last few evenings.

MRS. CRATCHIT
Oh I have known him walk, with Tiny Tim upon his shoulder, very fast indeed. He was very light to carry, and his father loved him so, it was no trouble. But there he is.

NARRATOR 1
His tea was ready for him on the hob, and they all tried who should help him to it most.

BOB CRATCHIT
Well look at the work upon this table! You'll be done long before Sunday.

MRS. CRATCHIT
You went again today, then, Robert?

BOB CRATCHIT
How green a place it is. But you'll see it often. I promised him that we would walk there on a Sunday.

NARRATOR 1
Bob told them of the extraordinary kindness of Mr. Scrooge's nephew Fred who, meeting him in the street that day, inquired.

BOB CRATCHIT
"I am 'eartily sorry for it," he said, "and sorry for your good wife." Although how he knew that I don't know.

MRS. CRATCHIT
Knew what, my dear?

BOB CRATCHIT
Why, that you were a good wife.

PETER
Everybody knows that, father!

BOB CRATCHIT
Well I hope they do, my boy. "If I can be of service to you in any way," he said, giving me his card, "that's where I live." It seemed almost as if he had known our Tiny Tim, and felt with us. And I shouldn't be at all surprised -- mark what I say -- if he got Peter a better situation!

MRS. CRATCHIT
'ear that, Peter!

MARTHA CRATCHIT
And then Peter will be keeping company with someone, and setting up house for himself!

All laugh in relief.

BOB CRATCHIT
It's as likely as not, one of these days. But however, and whenever we part from one another, we shall none of us forget Tiny Tim, or this first parting that there was among us. And when we recollect how patient and how mild he was, we shall not quarrel easily among ourselves, eh?

MRS. CRATCHIT
No never, father.

BOB CRATCHIT
I am very happy.

SOUND: BASS DRUM

NARRATOR 2
They reached an iron gate.

SCROOGE
Specter, something informs me that our parting moment is at hand.

NARRATOR 2
A churchyard, overrun by grass and weeds, choked up with too much burying. The Spirit stood among the graves, and pointed down to one.

SOUND: BASS DRUM

SCROOGE
Spirit, before I draw near the stone to which you point, one question. Are these the Shadows of Things that Will Be, or Shadows of Things that May Be? Men's courses will foreshadow certain ends to which, *if persevered in*, they must lead. But if the course be *departed from*, the ends will change. Say it is thus with what you show me!

SOUND: DRUM CONTINUES
"Ebenezer Scrooge!' Was I - am I that man? No, Spirit! No!

SOUND: WAILS AND CRIES
Spirit, hear me! I am not the man I was. I will not be the man I have been. I will honor Christmas, and keep it all the year. I will live in the Past, the Present, and the Future. The Spirits of all Three shall strive within me. Oh tell me I may sponge away the writing on this stone! Oh, Spirit!

SOUND: DRUM
He caught the spectral hand. The Phantom's hood and dress. It shrunk, collapsed, and dwindled down into…

SOUND OUT

SCROOGE
A bedpost! Mine own! Yes! This Bed is mine own! This Room. Best! The
Time before me is mine own, to make amends! I *will* live in the Past, the
Present, and the Future! The Spirits of all three shall strive within me. Oh,
Jacob Marley! Heaven and the Christmas Time be praised for this! Oh, I
don't know what to do! I'm light as a Feather. There's the door Jacob
entered! There's the corner where the Ghost sat! There's the window
where I saw the Spirits! It's all true! It all happened! Ha ha!

NARRATOR 2
It was a splendid laugh; an illustrious laugh; the Father of a long line of
Brilliant Laughs!

SCROOGE
I don't know what day it is. I don't know how long I've been among the
Spirits. I don't know anything. I'm quite a baby. Hallo!

SOUND: CHURCH BELLS JOYFUL

NARRATOR 1
He was checked by the churches ringing out the lustiest peals he had ever
heard. Clash, clang; ding dong bell!

SCROOGE
Glorious! Miss? Miss! What's today?

GIRL
Sir?

SCROOGE
What's today, my fine Miss?

GIRL
Why, Christmas Day!

SCROOGE
I haven't missed it! The Spirits have done it all in one night! Well, of
course! They can do anything they like. My girl, do you know the
Poulterers in the next street, at the corner?

GIRL
I should hope I did.

SCROOGE
A remarkable girl. My Miss, do you know whether they've sold the prize turkey that was hanging there?

GIRL
The one as big as me?

SCROOGE
Delightful miss! Yes!

GIRL
It's hanging there now.

SCROOGE
Go and buy it.

GIRL
Walker!

SCROOGE
Tell them to bring it here that I may give them direction where to take it. Come back with the man and I'll give you a shilling. In less than five minutes, a half-a-crown!

NARRATOR 2
The girl was off like a shot.

SCROOGE
I'll send it to Bob Cratchit's. He shan't know who sent it. It's twice the size of Tiny Tim. Tee hee.

NARRATOR 2
The Chuckle with which he said this; and the Chuckle with which he paid for the Turkey; and the Chuckle with which he paid for the Cab; and the Chuckle with which he recompensed the Boy; were

only to be exceeded by the Chuckle with which he sat in his Chair again, and Chuckled... till he Cried.

NARRATOR 1
He dressed himself all in his best, and at last got into the streets. The people were pouring forth, and Scrooge regarded every one with a delighted smile. He had not gone far when he beheld the good people who had walked into his counting-house the day before.

SCROOGE
My dear friends. A merry Christmas to you!

GOODMAN 2
Mr. Scrooge?

SCROOGE
That is my name. I fear it may not be pleasant to you. Allow me to ask your pardon. And would you have the goodness to take-- (Whispers.)

GOODMAN 1
Lord bless me! My dear Mr. Scrooge, are you serious? I don't know what to say to such munificence.

SCROOGE
Don't say anything. But -- come and see me? Will you come and see me? Thank you.

NARRATOR 1
He went to church, and watched the people, and patted children on the head. In the afternoon...

SOUND: WARM LAUGHTER

SCROOGE
Is your master at home, my dear?

SERVANT
Yes, sir. In the dining-room, sir, along with mistress.

SCROOGE
Thank you. He knows me. I'll go in. Fred?

FRED
Bless my soul.

SCROOGE
It's your Uncle Scrooge. I've come to dinner. Will you let me in,
Fred?

NARRATOR 1
Let him in? It's a mercy he didn't shake his arm off. He was at home
in five minutes. Wonderful party, wonderful games, wonderful
happiness.

BEAT.

SOUND: Dingalink

NARRATOR 2
Scrooge was early at the office next morning. If he could only be
there first, and catch Bob Cratchit coming late! The clock struck
nine. No Bob. Quarter past. No Bob.

SOUND: DINGALING!

SCROOGE
Sir! What do you mean by coming here at this time of day?

BOB CRATCHIT
I am very sorry, sir. I am...

SCROOGE
Step this way, sir, if you please.

BOB CRATCHIT
It's only once a year, sir.

SCROOGE
I am not going to stand this sort of thing any longer, sir. And therefore, Mr. Cratchit, I am afraid I must insist upon raising your salary! (Beat.) Merry Christmas, Bob. A merrier Christmas than I have given you for many a year. I will raise your salary, and assist your family, and we will discuss your affairs this very afternoon over a Christmas bowl. Now, Bob, I order you to make up the fires, and go buy another coal scuttle before you dot another "I".

SOUND: SILENT NIGHT (HUM)

NARRATOR 1
Scrooge was better than his word. He did it all and infinitely more. To Tiny Tim, who did not die, he was a Second Father. He became as good a Friend, as good a Master, as good a Man, as the good old city knew. He had no further intercourse with Spirits, but lived upon the Total Abstinence Principle ever afterwards. And it was always said of him that he knew how to keep Christmas well. May that be truly said of us, and all of us.

NARRATOR 2
And so, as Tiny Tim observed ...

CAST
God bless Us. Every. One.

THE END

Made in United States
Orlando, FL
23 October 2023

38167340R00036